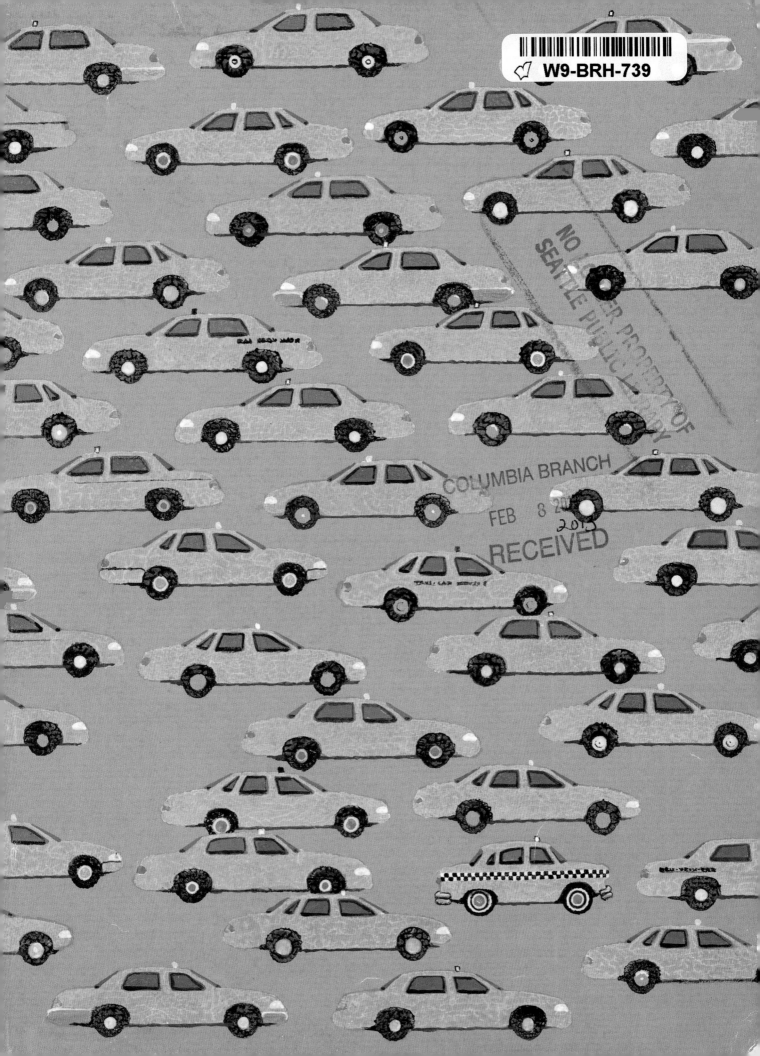

Distributed in the United States by NorthSouth Books Inc., New York 10016.
Library of Congress Cataloging-in-Publication Data is available.
Printed in Germany by Grafisches Centrum Cuno GmbH & Co. KG, 39240 Calbe, November 2012.
ISBN: 978-0-7358-4111-6
1 3 5 7 9 • 10 8 6 4 2
www.northsouth.com
Meet Marcus Pfister at www.marcuspfister.ch

FSC
www.fsc.org
MIX
Paper from
responsible sources
FSC® C043106

The Yellow Cab

MARCUS PFISTER

North South

Jack, the yellow cab, lived in a big city. There were thousands of yellow cabs in town. But no one knew the city quite like Jack did. He knew every corner, every building, and every street, no matter how small.

Once upon a time, Jack had whizzed through the streets as though he had wings, admired by all. These days, however, his wheels turned a little slower.

One day around lunchtime, Jack was out on one of the major thoroughfares. The cars stood in lines, bumper to bumper, inching forward.

Directly in front of him was a grumbling, foul-smelling bus. There was a glossy advertisement poster stuck to its rear window. **COME TO BRAZIL!** Jack read. The image was of brightly colored flowers and birds in a lush rain forest.

"That looks like paradise!" thought Jack with a dreamy sigh.

Jack could not take his eyes off the poster. All of a sudden it was as if he had wings again! He felt as he had all those years ago, when everyone had looked at him in awe. Turning at the next intersection, Jack took the long bridge out of town.

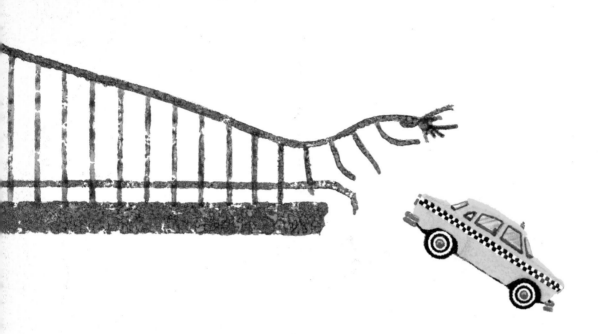

But what was this? With no warning, the bridge suddenly gave way to a precipice. Had he missed some barrier or detour?

There was no time to brake. Jack plummeted downward!

Until, that is, the yellow cab opened his doors like wings and gently sailed along—onward and ever onward, over a vast expanse of forest.

This surely was the rain forest!

Three red parrots became his flying companions. They gazed in amazement at the yellow flying object. Approaching a forest glade, they landed together.

There were ferns, plants, and flowers everywhere: a blaze of shimmering color.

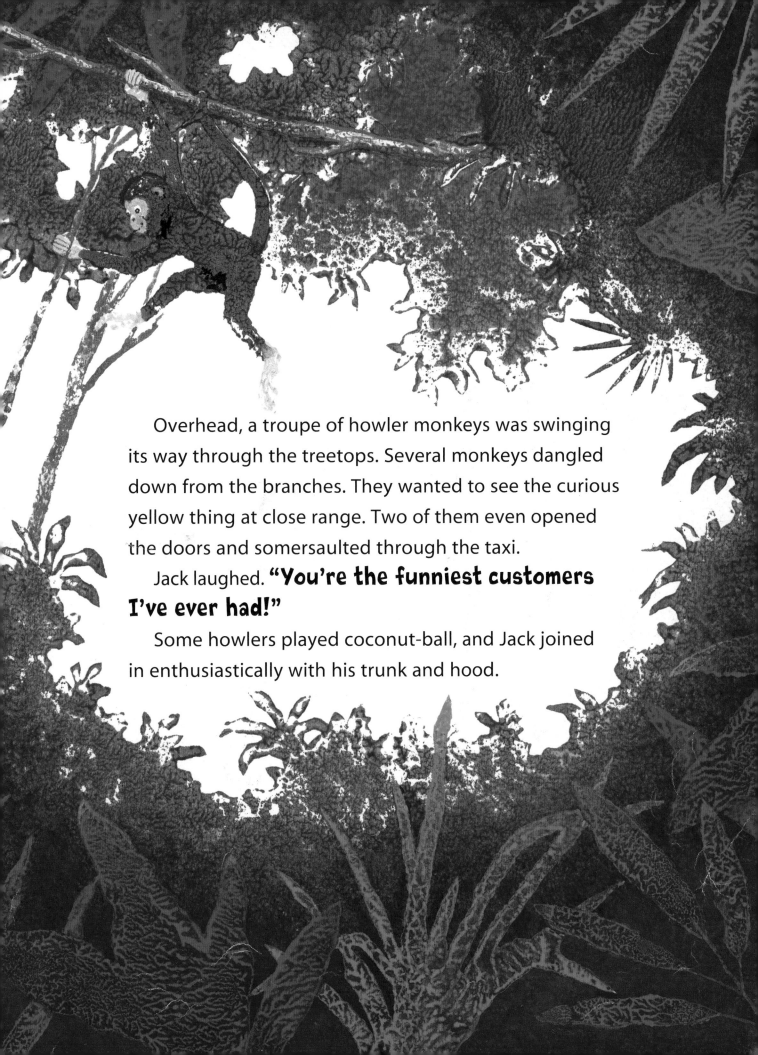

Overhead, a troupe of howler monkeys was swinging its way through the treetops. Several monkeys dangled down from the branches. They wanted to see the curious yellow thing at close range. Two of them even opened the doors and somersaulted through the taxi.

Jack laughed. **"You're the funniest customers I've ever had!"**

Some howlers played coconut-ball, and Jack joined in enthusiastically with his trunk and hood.

Jack discovered more and more animals. Many were camouflaged and hard to spot. That was especially true of the chameleon. He blended in perfectly with his surroundings, and Jack only noticed him by chance. As he approached, the creature changed color—all gleaming yellow like a miniature taxi!

Suddenly, however, the birds took flight as if on command. The howler monkeys, too, disappeared into the treetops.

Jack could hear a deep rumbling—a noise that grew louder and louder.

A gigantic yellow excavator burst into view through the undergrowth, with two other construction vehicles in tow.

Jack was furious. Those three had frightened off all of the animals!

His curiosity was roused, and he followed behind. They were sort of distant relatives, after all. What on Earth were they doing here in the rain forest?

The trucks and Jack reached an ugly, wide scar of a road.

The entire section of forest had been laid bare and flattened. And the three gigantic excavators were about to cut down even more trees.

Jack was numb with horror. He couldn't believe it. His own relatives were destroying this paradise!

Without stopping to think, he placed himself in their path. **"Are you crazy?"** Jack yelled. **"What are you doing?"**

The machines turned off their engines reluctantly.

"What does it look like?" one of the excavators snarled. **"We're cutting down trees! This will be a road. And we're clearing the way for a massive field of soybeans."**

"A soybean field? But all the animals and plants—what about them?" shouted Jack in despair.

"Animals? I haven't seen a single one—ever," growled the excavator in his gravelly voice.

One by one the animals appeared in the clearing.

A few cheeky monkeys leaped up onto the machines.

"Hey, that tickles!" snorted the scoop-nosed digger, lifting and lowering the monkeys on his shovel. They screeched with delight.

Then Jack had an idea.

"Listen up, you yellow giants," he said. **"The place I'm from needs lots of construction—there are streets, schools, and great big playgrounds to be built. Wouldn't that be smarter than tearing up this forest, which is quite unique?!"**

The excavators liked the sound of this. They did not care for the rain forest's humid climate. Their yellow paint was beginning to flake. And so they followed the little yellow cab back to the city.

As if by magic, more and more construction machines joined the strange procession. And out of the forest they went, each and every one.

The convoy drew to a halt by a traffic light. A regular symphony of hooting horns came from behind. Jack was jolted out of his dream—but the beeping and honking continued. He must have dozed off at the traffic light. A long line had formed behind him. The bus in front had long since gone.

Jack started his engine and chugged off. What an incredible dream that had been!

Passing by a huge construction site, he couldn't believe his eyes—there, hard at work, were the very construction machines he had guided out of the rain forest in his dream. All three of them! And when the large excavator gave a jaunty wave with his shovel, Jack nearly knocked over a no-entry blockade.

Jack drove on happily. He checked his back mirror once more and gasped in amazement—there on the backseat lay . . . a coconut.

Why is a rain forest called a "rain forest"?

A forest is classified as a rain forest if it gets at least 68 to 78 inches of rain a year. (That's enough water to fill a 5-to-6-foot-deep swimming pool over your entire town!)

Why are rain forests important?

Rain forests help clean the air we breathe, and many of our medicines have been (and are still being) discovered there.

Where are rain forests located?

Tropical rain forests are located near the equator and have warm, tropical climates. The largest tract of tropical rain forest is located in the Amazon Basin in South America. About 60 percent of this rain forest is located in Brazil.

Why are the tropical rain forests at risk?

Our tropical rain forests are at risk because of climate changes and because of the activities that people are doing, such as cutting down trees for wood, clearing forests for grazing cattle, and cutting down trees to grow crops such as soy beans.